Kai THE DANCING Butterfly

Story by
Crystal Z. Lee

Illustrations by
Allie Su

balestierpress

For Christabelle and Gabriella,

may you fly with faith.

Balestier Press
Centurion House, London TW18 4AX
www.balestier.com

Kai the Dancing Butterfly
Copyright © 2022 by Balestier Press
Story by Crystal Z. Lee
Illustrations by Allie Su

First published by Balestier Press in 2022

A CIP catalogue record for this book is available from the British Library.

ISBN 978 1 913891 17 6 (hardcover)
ISBN 978 1 913891 18 3 (pbk.)

For
Children Everywhere
and for
Friends of Taiwan

My name is Kai. I am a purple butterfly. My home is in Taiwan, a beautiful island also known as the Butterfly Kingdom.

I am preparing for the biggest trip
of the year: the journey from the
northern tip of the island,
to Maolin in the south.

That is a long way to fly!
I'll need to make some
stops along the way.

My sister, Ami, is older and bigger than me. She is the star of the Maolin Winter Festival dance show.

I'm nervous about the journey. I've never flown so far before.

"C'mon, follow me!" my sister says.
We perch on Queen's Head Rock overlooking the ocean, where we spent our summer.
We bid goodbye to the birds, then we're off!

We gaze at the sunrise from Cape Santiago Lighthouse before getting a drink near Golden Waterfall.

We pass by Red Hair Fort, enjoy the art at Yingge Ceramics Street, fly over Freedom Square, then land near the tallest building in Taiwan, Taipei 101.

Next, we stop by Tashee Blooming Oasis. We're hungry! Luckily for us, this flower farm is full of delicious nectar. My sister starts practicing her dance routine. She shows me the Blooming Ballet moves. It looks graceful, and difficult.

"Kai, now you try," she says.
"But my legs are tiny. I'm not sure if I can do it," I say worriedly.
"You won't know until you try," says Ami. She demonstrates the ballet twirls again.
I try to follow her. "That's it! You've got it," she cheers.

We fly past Yimin Temple, then stop by to say hello to the monkeys at Tai'an Hot Springs.

We're thirsty! We take a drink near Seven Homes Creek, then play with our salmon friends.

Our fish friends give us directions to our next stop: Taroko Gorge.
I follow my sister as we make our way to Swallow Grotto.
Ami shows me the Swallow Swing Dance moves. It looks fun, and complicated.

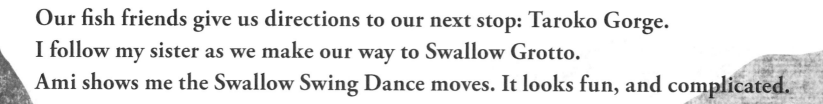

"Kai, your turn," she says.
"But my wings are short.
I doubt I can dance like that,"
I say.

"Just try your best," she replies.
Ami flutters around me in her swing dance
routine as I try my best to follow along.
"Nice moves, Kai! I like that you're putting
your own spin on it," she cheers.

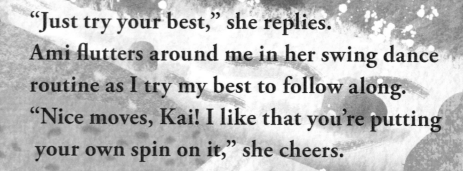

Past the Women's Hope Church, the Taroko Gorge Music Festival is happening near the Bilu Sacred Tree.

We dance to the music with many creatures, including owls, geckos, magpies, macaques, pangolins, pheasants, tree frogs, jewel beetles, and sika deers.

My sister teaches all of us the Formosa Flutter dance!

We fly past the Ox Ear sculptures, pat the golden hen, then pause near Sun Moon Lake for a drink.

We pay our respects to the white deer and to Xuanzang the monk. Then we land at the Mercy Blessing Pagoda and play with our firefly friends!

Arriving in the oldest city on the island, we admire the historic architecture of Anping Old Fort and Chihkan Tower.

We pass by the Confucius Temple before making our way to the salt fields. We have a splendid time dancing at the Salt for Peace Festival!

We love the autumn leaves and colors in the Alishan Forest!
We enjoy some High Mountain Tea before Ami teaches me her
Wandering Wind moves.

"You're really finding your rhythm, Kai!"
says Ami.

I'm so focused on the routine that I'm soon out of breath. I land on a fuzzy large rock, resting my wings.

Suddenly, the rock starts moving!

"Kai!" Ami screams.

"You're on the nose of a Taiwanese black bear!"

The bear smiles. "Hi, I'm Taya, and this is my friend, Lan the leopard. Can you teach us to dance like that?" We demonstrate the dance, and prance in the forest with them.

But the weather is getting colder, so we must be on our way. "We can lead you to Maolin," Taya and Lan say. "Let's go!"

With Taya and Lan as our guides, we fly through
the forests of Taiwan Central Mountain Range
and pass by trees that reach the moon.

Sometimes we take a break to
practice our dance moves,
sometimes we rest on their backs
as they hike.

After many days, Taya and Lan say we are almost there. "You just need to cross this Butterfly Highway, then you will reach your destination!" they say. We look at the netted bridge forming an arch along the road. All kinds of cars zoom past us. "Won't you come with us?" we ask.
"This highway is for butterflies only," they reply.
"We'll meet you at the festival later!"

We watch as some other purple butterflies fly through the Butterfly Highway.
We fluff our wings, then we soar along with them.

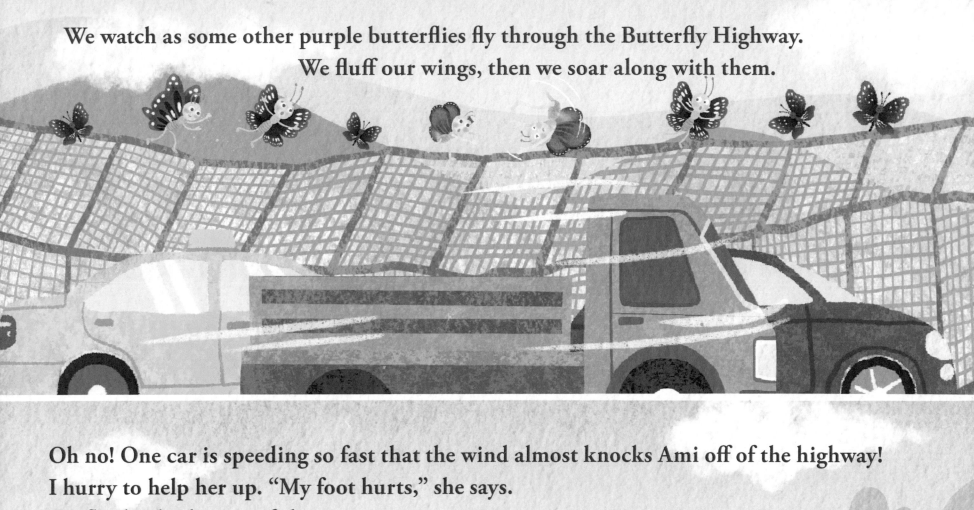

Oh no! One car is speeding so fast that the wind almost knocks Ami off of the highway!
I hurry to help her up. "My foot hurts," she says.
We fly slowly the rest of the way.

We finally reach Maolin!
Everybody is preparing for the
Winter Festival dance show.

"Kai," my sister says, "you must take my place in the show." She rubs her feet.

"I can't! I'm not ready!"

"Yes you are, Kai. I've seen you practice. Now repeat after me: I can do this."

"I can do this," I say slowly but surely.

"That's right! Remember, you're a star!" Ami says.

My sister helps me onto the stage. I watch the sun setting in the distance as the clouds turn pink, a cue for the audience to find their seats. I take a deep breath.

As the music swells, I begin with the Blooming Ballet moves. When the melody quickens, I soar into the Swallow Swing Dance.

Next, I fly into the Formosa Flutter routine, then glide into the Wandering Wind moves. The audience marvels at the way my wings and outfits transform as I dance.

When the music crescendos, I leap into the air under the full moon, and finish the performance with a Kai Moonwalk, a dance move I choreographed myself.

"Bravo! You did it!" my sister shouts excitedly, as Taya and Lan wave from the audience. "WE did it!" I shout back, as everybody claps and cheers!

Message from the Author

Taiwan is often called the "Butterfly Kingdom," because it is home to more than 400 species of butterflies, 50 of which are endemic to the island. Taiwan is also home to one of the planet's two mass butterfly overwintering congregations, the other being the monarch butterflies that migrate to Mexico. Every winter, hundreds of thousands of Taiwan's purple crow butterflies travel hundreds of kilometers to Maolin National Scenic Area, making their way to the Dawu mountain foothills. The phenomenon creates a magnificent purple butterfly valley!

Many Indigenous tribes in Taiwan have revered butterflies for centuries, and butterfly symbols can be found on their traditional garments and ornaments. Taiwan was inhabited by Aboriginal people for thousands of years before the major Han immigration of the seventeenth century. Currently, 16 Indigenous tribes in Taiwan are officially recognized. In this book, the following Indigenous tribes are mentioned, or their traditional attire is featured in the illustrations: Paiwan, Tsou, Thao, Siraya, Atayal, Kavalan, Truku, Rukai, and the Amis. Today, more than half a million Taiwanese Aboriginal people live in Taiwan.

Did you know that all butterflies have six legs? However the purple crow butterfly is categorized as brush-footed or four-footed, because they stand on four legs while the other two legs are curled up and may not be easily visible. The illustrations in this book also include many of Taiwan's other unique animals, such as egrets, grass owls, tree frogs, jewel beetles, black-faced spoonbills. Animals native to Taiwan featured here include the Formosan sika deer, the Taiwanese pangolin, the Kikuchi's Gecko, the Taiwan blue magpie, the Formosan clouded leopard, the Mikado pheasant, the Formosan rock macaque, the Taiwanese black bear, and the Formosan landlocked salmon. Some of these majestic species are unfortunately, critically endangered. The purple crow butterfly population numbers have also been decreasing, prompting the Taiwanese government to strengthen conservation efforts, such as installing nets over highways to protect the butterflies from vehicles. Next time you see these purple wayfarers in Taiwan, remember to root them on because they might have traveled a very long way!

We hope this story will spark an interest in learning more about Taiwan's history, its rich biodiversity, its fascinating flora and fauna, its spectacular natural scenery, and its incredible Indigenous cultures. By featuring some of Taiwan's at-risk or endangered species in this book, our goal is to bring more awareness around animal habitat protection and ecological conservation.

Glossary

Queen's Head Rock (野柳女王頭)
Located at Yehliu Geopark in New Taipei, Queen's Head Rock is a sandstone formation sculpted naturally by wind and sea water. It is famous for resembling the bust of a crowned lady. Yehliu Geopark also attracts many birdwatching enthusiasts.

Sandiaojiao Lighthouse (三貂角燈塔)
Also named "Cape Santiago," this lighthouse in New Taipei is often called "the eye of Taiwan." It sits on the island's easternmost tip, and is an ideal place to catch the dawn's first rays to shine on Taiwan.

Golden Waterfall (金瓜石黃金瀑布)
Golden Waterfall is part of the Jinguashi Geological Park in New Taipei. As elements from abandoned gold and copper mines interact with water dropping from the sharp terrain, it creates the sight of a gold-colored waterfall. Translated literally, Jinguashi means "golden melon stone." This area was once the center of a gold rush and considered the most profitable mining site in Asia. Jinguashi was especially heavily mined during the Japanese occupation.

Fort San Domingo (淡水紅毛城)
Also called "Tamsui Hongmao Fortress," its Chinese name means "red hair fort." First built nearly 400 years ago during the Spanish occupation, the fort was later re-built during the Dutch colonization. The Taiwanese called the Dutch "an mo," or "red hair people." Located in New Taipei, this historic piece of architecture features Spanish, Dutch and British influences.

Yingge Ceramics Town (鶯歌老街)
Yingge is the pottery capital of Taiwan, and the history of ceramics production there dates back over 200 years ago. Now there are over 800 ceramics-related businesses at Yingge in New Taipei.

Freedom Square (自由廣場)

This public plaza is home to several landmarks: National Theater, Chiang Kai-shek Memorial, National Concert Hall. Located in Taipei city, the capital of Taiwan, the square is within sight of the Presidential Office.

Taipei101 (台北101)

Seen as a symbol of Taiwan, this skyscraper soars 101 floors above ground. Taipei101 is considered one of the world's tallest "green buildings," that is, the structure is a model for energy efficiency, and was designed and built with environmentally-responsible resources and applications.

Tashee Blooming Oasis (大溪花海)

Located in Taoyuan municipality, this farm is a popular filming site for Taiwanese dramas because of its rolling flower fields and gardens. A section of the farm was formerly a tea factory cultivating Assam and matcha tea.

Yimin Temple (褒忠亭義民廟)

First built over 200 years ago, Yimin Temple is an important Hakka religious center found in Hsinchu county.

Tai'an Hot Springs (泰安溫泉)

This thermal hot springs is located in Miaoli county and is said to have been treasured by the Indigenous Atayal tribe for its skincare benefits.

Qijiawan Creek (七家灣溪)

Qijiawan is located in the Taichung city section of Shei-Pa National Park. Translated literally, Qijiawan means "seven homes creek." This creek is home to the Formosan Landlocked Salmon, an endangered fish species found only in Taiwan.

Swallow Grotto (燕子口)

River erosion among the marble cliff faces have resulted in natural carved wonders at the Swallow Grotto section of Taroko National Park. Pacific swallows build nests on the rock walls, giving the geological phenomenon its name.

Taroko Gorge (太魯閣)

Named after the Indigenous Truku tribe, Taroko National Park is known for its towering marble canyons. The park is home to a wide range of ecosystems, from torrential rivers, forested trails, to bamboo fields, coastal cliffs, and snow-peaked mountains. Most of Taiwan's animal species can be found here. The park spans Hualien, Taichung, and Nantou counties.

Ciwang Memorial Church (姬望紀念教會)

In one of the translations, Ciwang can mean "women's hope." Located in Hualien, this church was named after Ciwang Iwal, a woman from the Truku Indigenous tribe. She is revered for establishing a Christian church specifically for Taiwanese Aboriginal people even in the face of Japanese colonial opposition during the 1930s.

Bilu Sacred Tree (碧綠神木)

Found near Mount Hehuan in Taroko National Park, the Bilu Sacred Tree is a native Taiwanese tree species that is over 3,200 years old.

New Era Sculpture Park (牛耳藝術渡假村)

This art park is located in Nantou and comprises of many sculptural creations by three Taiwanese artists who were all born in the Year of the Ox. Hence the park is also named Niu'er, meaning "ox ear."

Zinan Temple (紫南宮)

Established over 270 years ago, Zinan temple in Nantou has since become famous among the Taiwanese as an institution to borrow funds. Locals believe patting the giant golden hen sculpture will bring good fortune. On Lunar New Year's Day the temple distributes lucky coins which are believed to invite prosperity.

Sun Moon Lake (日月潭)

Located in Nantou, Sun Moon Lake is Taiwan's largest alpine lake. Its surrounding area was first inhabited by the Indigenous Thao tribe. Visitors can take the cable car from the base of the lake to the Formosan Aboriginal Culture Village.

Lalu Island (拉魯島)

Lalu Island sits in Sun Moon Lake and is considered sacred ground for the Indigenous Thao tribe. There is a legend about a white deer which led the Thao Aboriginal people to discover Sun Moon Lake. A sculpture of a white deer can be found on Lalu Island.

Xuanzang Temple (玄奘寺)

Built with Tang dynasty architectural elements, this temple overlooks Sun Moon Lake and houses some relics of Xuanzang, a Buddhist monk who traveled between China and India about 1,500 years ago. The pilgrimage inspired the novel *Journey to the West*, considered a classic in Chinese literature.

Ci'en Pagoda (慈恩塔)

Translated literally, Ci'en can mean "mercy and blessings" or "mother's mercy." It's an ideal place to admire sweeping vistas of Sun Moon Lake and spot fireflies.

Chihkan Tower (赤崁樓)

This fortress was first built over 350 years ago during the Dutch colonization of Formosa (the former name of Taiwan). Located in Tainan municipality, Chihkan Tower was named after "Sakam," the Indigenous Siraya village in the area.

Anping Old Fort (安平古堡)

A prominent historic landmark in Tainan, this fort was built nearly 400 years ago during the Dutch occupation. Later the fortress became a base for Koxinga (also known as Zheng Chenggong), a Ming dynasty Chinese loyalist who defeated and ended the Dutch colonization of Formosa.

Confucius Temple (全臺首學台南孔廟)

Built over 350 years ago, this temple in Tainan was established in reverence of Confucius, and has been used as an educational academy.

Kungshen Wangye Salt For Peace Festival (鯤鯓王平安鹽祭)

This festival celebrates Taoist beliefs, folk performances, salt industry programs, and is held at the 300-year-old Nankunshen Daitian Temple in Tainan city. The Taiwanese salt industry has thrived in Tainan for centuries. Traditionally, filling a pouch with salt and rice at the "sprinkling ceremony" is said to ward off evil spirits and bring peace.

Cigu District (七股)

Cigu is located in southwestern Tainan and is famous for its salt production, as well as attractions such as the Cigu Salt Mountain and the Taiwan Salt Activity Village. Cigu's other claim to fame is its wetlands, an ecological reserve and haven for the endangered black-faced spoonbills.

Alishan National Forest Recreation Area (阿里山國家森林遊樂區)

Alishan, or Mount Ali, is located in Chiayi county, and was first settled by the Tsou Indigenous tribe. Along with its magnificent wildlife and woodlands, Alishan is also famous for its locomotives and High Mountain Tea.

Taiwan Central Mountain Range (台灣中央山脈)

Taiwan Spruce is endemic to the island and can be found in its Central Mountain Range. Taiwania is an ancient coniferous tree species and one of the tallest in Asia. Rukai Aboriginal people called them "the trees that hit the moon." Taiwan Central Mountain Range runs from the north of the island in Yilan to the southernmost tip in Pingtung.

Butterfly Highway (紫斑蝶防護網)

To protect the purple crow butterflies, the Taiwanese government created the world's first "butterfly highway." The nets installed over freeways encourage the butterflies to fly higher, avoiding collision with vehicles. In some cases, the government had closed major highways to help safe passage of the butterflies during their seasonal migrations.

Maolin National Scenic Area (茂林國家風景區)

Located in Kaohsiung and Pingtung counties, the Maolin National Scenic Area is home to millions of overwintering butterflies. This area is also the ancestral land for many Rukai Aboriginal people. Duona High Suspension Bridge can be found here and is decorated with Indigenous Rukai totems.

Author's Note

There is usually more than one way to spell Chinese to English translations. Most of the sites and monuments mentioned in this book are referenced by the name that is more widely known. For example, the alternative spelling for Xuanzang is Syuentzang. I used "Xuanzang Temple" since that is the spelling adopted by the Taiwan Tourism Bureau. In other instances, I exercised creative liberty for this fictional tale and penned names to further the whimsicality of the story. For example, I chose the name "Red Hair Fort" for Fort San Domingo, since that is the popular nickname locals use for the monument. The glossary provides factual, albeit brief information on each location featured in this story, including a sprinkling of Taiwanese history, such as mentions of colonization and occupation. This is a story of resilience, tenacity, and transformation. The same virtues can be said of the Taiwanese spirit!

About the Author

Crystal Z. Lee was raised in a bilingual household in Taiwan and in California. Her great-grandparents and grandparents are originally from Taichung, Hualien, and Jinguashi area in Taipei. Crystal grew up in Taipei, and later returned to live there in her adult years. Some of her favorite memories in Taiwan include lighting lanterns with her family in Pingxi, attending a school field trip in Yehliu, boating at Sun Moon Lake, dining at grand banquets with relatives, hiking at Yangming mountain with her parents, sampling every boba tea possible with her sister, taking wedding photographs in Tamsui, and even giving birth to her child in Taipei! Her young children love dancing and adore butterflies, and have been learning how to grow plants that are beneficial for butterflies. Crystal is also the author of the children's book *A Unicorn Named Rin*, and the novel, *Love and Other Moods*.

About the Illustrator

Allie Su was born and raised in Yunlin county, Taiwan. She attended Nanhua University in Chiayi city, majoring in Visual Arts. She is a professional illustrator, specializing in oil painting and ink painting. Allie adores vegetarian food and hot coffee. She believes in bringing joy to people worldwide through art.

CPSIA information can be obtained
at www.ICGtesting.com
Printed in the USA
LVRC100926050422
715343LV00010B/288